#03
Pio Pico/Koreatown Branch
694 S. Oxford Avenue
Los Angeles, CA 90005

THE ELEMENTS

Arsenic

Chris Cooper

mc **Marshall Cavendish**
Benchmark
New York

Marshall Cavendish Benchmark
99 White Plains Road
Tarrytown, New York 10591

www.marshallcavendish.us

Library of Congress Cataloging-in-Publication Data

Cooper, Chris
Arsenic / Chris Cooper.
    p.   cm. — (The elements)
Includes index.
ISBN-13: 978-0-7614-2203-7
ISBN-10: 0-7614-2203-X
1. Arsenic—Juvenile literature. 2. Chemical elements—Juvenile literature.
I. Title. II. Series: Elements (Marshall Cavendish Benchmark)

QD181.A7C66 2007
546'.715—dc22

2006043891

1 6 5 4 3 2

Printed in Malaysia

Picture credits
Front cover: Corbis
Back cover: Science Photo Library

Stan Celestain: 9
Corbis: Lester V. Bergman 4t, Michael Freeman 21, Antoine Gyori 4–5,
Reuters 26, Reuters/Sucheta Das 24, Zefa/A. Fichte 14
Getty Images: Hulton 12
Mary Evans Picture Library: 13
Photos.com: 1, 20, 30
Science & Society Picture Library: Science Museum 25, Science Museum Pictorial 10
Science Photo Library: Klaus Guldbrandsen 7, Manfred Kage 15, Mike McNamee 22, Hank Morgan 23,
STC/A. Sternberg 6, Sinclair Stammers 8, Andrew Syred 3, 17, 18, Sheila Terry 11

Series created by The Brown Reference Group plc.
Designed by Sarah Williams
www.brownreference.com

Contents

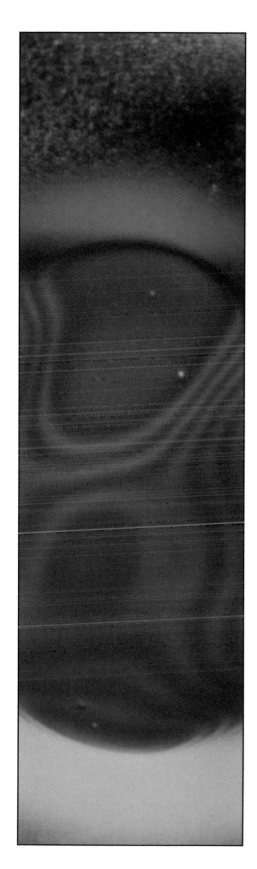

What is arsenic?

Although arsenic is not a rare element, most people will never see it. It is a very dangerous substance, whether on its own or combined with other elements, and the public is safeguarded from coming into contact with it. Arsenic is famous as a poison. It has often been used by murderers in the past, both in real life and in stories. However, arsenic is also used in medicines.

Arsenic is a metalloid. It is shiny like a metal but crumbles into a powder like a nonmetal. Gray arsenic is the most common form of the element.

The uses of arsenic

Pure arsenic is a shiny silver-gray solid material. It is used in a wide variety of ways. For example, when arsenic is mixed with metals, it makes the metals harder. Arsenic is also one of several materials used in microchips for electronic devices, such as computers and cell phones. Arsenic is also sometimes used to make smoke and flashes in fireworks and for making clear glass. As a powerful poison, arsenic is used against rats and other animals considered to be pests.

The usefulness of arsenic comes from its chemical behavior—the way in which its atoms join with each other or with atoms of other elements. Atoms are the smallest units of an element. They are tiny—100

million of them side by side would stretch across the width of a fingernail. However, atoms are made up of even smaller particles.

Inside atoms

Most of the material in an atom is packed into a tiny central core called the nucleus. The nucleus contains two types of particles: protons and neutrons. Protons have a positive electric charge. Neutrons are slightly heavier than protons and have no electric charge—they are neutral.

A third kind of particle, the electrons, move around the nucleus. Electrons have about two-thousandth of the mass of a proton or neutron. However, they have a negative charge that is equal but opposite to the positive charge of the protons.

All atoms have an equal number of electrons and protons. The opposite charges balance each other out, and the atom has no overall charge. Positive charges repel or push away other positive charges, but attract negative charges. The positively charged nucleus

Pure arsenic and many of its compounds are very poisonous. The soil in this town in the Ural Mountains of Russia has been polluted with arsenic and other dangerous elements released from factories.

pulls on the negatively charged electrons. This force—called electromagnetism— keeps the atom together.

The arsenic atom

What makes an element different from all other elements is the number of protons in its atoms. The nucleus of an arsenic atom contains 33 protons. Scientists describe this as an atomic number of 33.

There are also 42 neutrons in the nucleus, so the total number of protons and neutrons in the nucleus is 75. This is the atomic mass number of arsenic.

The arsenic atom has 33 electrons circling the nucleus. The electrons interact with the electrons of other atoms. The way they do this gives arsenic its unique physical and chemical properties.

Special characteristics

Arsenic atoms combine with each other in different ways to make different forms of arsenic. The usual form is a gray, shiny

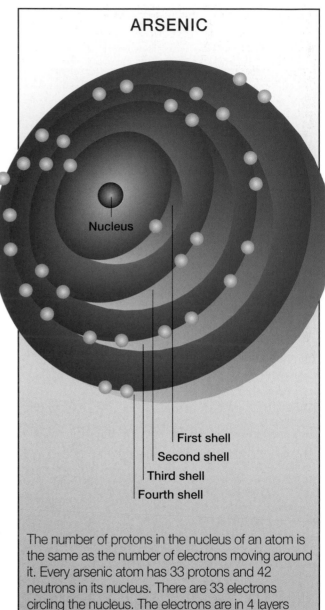

ARSENIC

Nucleus

First shell
Second shell
Third shell
Fourth shell

The number of protons in the nucleus of an atom is the same as the number of electrons moving around it. Every arsenic atom has 33 protons and 42 neutrons in its nucleus. There are 33 electrons circling the nucleus. The electrons are in 4 layers called electron shells. There are 2 electrons in the inner shell, 8 electrons in the second shell, 18 electrons in the third shell, and 5 in the outer shell.

Arsenic is an important component in microchips. This is a close up of a circuit made with gallium arsenide. This arsenic compound is a semiconductor. Semiconductors are used to make tiny switches and other components for machines such as computers.

substance. However, there is also a yellow form, which easily turns into the gray form. In the yellow form of arsenic, clusters of four arsenic atoms form a tetrahedron— a pyramid with four triangular faces. Yellow arsenic is chemically the same as gray arsenic, but it is much less dense.

Arsenic's less common form is known as yellow arsenic. It is much less dense than gray arsenic and is a bright yellow and very crumbly substance. The name arsenic comes from "zarnika," a Persian word meaning "golden."

A handful of gray arsenic weighs two and a half times as much as the same amount of yellow arsenic.

Arsenic is a metalloid, or semimetal. Metalloids are substances that have a mixture of properties. Some of these make the substance look and behave like a metal, while others make the element more like a nonmetal. For example, gray arsenic is like a metal, while yellow arsenic is more similar to a nonmetal.

ARSENIC FACTS

- Chemical symbol: As
- Atomic number: 33
- Atomic mass number: 75
- Melting point: 1503 °F (817 °C)
- Boiling point: 1137 °F (614 °C)
- Density (gray arsenic)   5.7 grams per cubic cm (5.7 times that of water)

Where arsenic is found

The shiny silver-gray crystals in this piece of rock are arsenopyrite. This is the most common arsenic mineral. It is often found with metal ores.

Pure arsenic is found in small amounts, but most of it is found combined with the atoms of other elements. When atoms of different elements combine, they form substances called compounds. Compounds often have very different properties from those of their individual ingredients. Natural compounds are known as minerals. There are several common arsenic minerals.

Rocks and minerals are not the same thing. A mineral is made of one chemical substance. A rock is normally made of several different minerals. Often the rock is made up of grains of the different minerals mixed up with each other. If a rock contains large amounts of useful minerals, is is called an ore.

Smelly mineral

The main arsenic-containing mineral is arsenopyrite (also called mispickel), in which arsenic is combined with iron and sulfur. It is a grayish white material that shines like a metal. When this mineral is broken up it produces a smell that is similar to garlic. Arsenopyrite is often found with other minerals that contain gold, silver, and other valuable metals. Arsenic is obtained when the rocks containing these minerals are refined.

Most arsenic is obtained as a byproduct when rock containing other metals is processed. Because it is so poisonous, arsenic is removed from waste materials produced by industry in most countries. The arsenic collected in this way is more than enough for the world's needs.

Gold substitute

Orpiment is another arsenic mineral, in which arsenic is combined with sulfur. Like arsenopyrite, it is often found with gold-containing minerals. Orpiment has a rich, deep yellow color. Powdered orpiment was used as a yellow pigment (coloring material) for many hundreds of years. The name *orpiment* comes from Latin meaning "gold pigment."

However, orpiment is very poisonous and it also discolored the other pigments that artists used. By the nineteenth century, the mineral was replaced by newly invented pigments, such as cadmium yellow. This combination of cadmium and sulfur was much less poisonous.

Realgar is another arsenic-containing mineral. It is arsenic sulfide (As_4S_4) like orpiment, but the crystals are arranged in a different way. Because of this arrangement, realgar is soft and reddish orange. Realgar often forms as large flat crystals. These were once carved into Chinese ornaments. Unfortunately, these did not usually last very long, because the mineral breaks down into other substances after being exposed to sunlight.

Realgar (above) is a red arsenic-containing mineral. Its name comes from the Arabic for "mine powder." Powdered realgar was once used to make red paint.

Orpiment (left) is another arsenic mineral. It is similar to realgar and was also used in paints and dyes. However, it is too poisonous to be used in this way today.

The history of arsenic

Bronze was the first metal that human beings learned to make. It consists of copper combined with small amounts of other elements, such as tin and arsenic. Bronze was very valuable in the ancient world for making weapons, ornaments, and mirrors. Arsenic compounds were therefore first used for making bronze. They have also been used as yellow and red dyes for many years.

Death sentence

The Greek geographer and historian Strabo, who lived about 2,000 years ago, described the arsenic mines that operated in his day. Strabo says that the workers in the mines were slaves who had committed serious crimes. As well as suffering from the hard work, arsenic miners were made ill by the arsenic-rich dust inside the mine. Most died of poisoning after a short while.

Magical ingredient

Arsenic compounds were also highly important in alchemy. Alchemy was a magical craft that began thousands of years ago in Egypt and China, and later spread to Greece. It spread across Europe in the twelfth century. Alchemists tried to make magical substances. They tried to create an elixir, which was a drink that would stop people from growing old. The

Albertus Magnus is thought to be the first person to produce pure arsenic. He was interested in alchemy but was one of the first people to use a scientific method to investigate nature. Magnus was also a religious leader and was made a saint in 1931.

panacea was a substance that cured all illnesses. They also tried to make a philosopher's stone, which could transform any metal into gold. Alchemists used a range of chemical techniques, including mixing, boiling, and dissolving materials.

Alchemists were the first people to investigate how substances reacted and combined with each other. They believed that arsenic was a basic ingredient in nearly all substances.

It was not the strangeness of their ideas that made the alchemists unscientific, but the fact that they did not systematically test those ideas and cooperate to build up knowledge. They described their activities and their results in a strange, symbolic language. This was more designed to impress outsiders and conceal information rather than to reveal it. Nevertheless, scientific chemistry grew from alchemy.

The alchemists did not use many of the ideas of modern chemistry. For example, alchemists did not understand about the elements and chemical reactions. They also did not distinguish between compounds, in which the atoms are bonded together, and mixtures, in which things were mixed together but still stay as separate substances.

The Arab alchemist Jabir ibn Hayyan (called Geber by some) considered minerals to be composed of "spirits" and metals. The metals were gold, silver, copper, and so on, while the spirits included sulfur, mercury, and arsenic. Geber claimed that pure gold contained only sulfur and

DID YOU KNOW?

Although chemistry and alchemy are both concerned with how natural materials are formed and can be changed into new materials, the two subjects are really quite different. Chemists are scientists. They investigate the elements and their compounds using experiments that can be repeated and checked by other chemists. Alchemists were more like magicians. The things that people now associate with wizards, such as bubbling potions with strange ingredients, are inspired by the work of alchemists.

It is very hard to know how much alchemists understood about the nature of the substances they were using. They did not record their ideas in a clear way. Geber was especially bad at this. His writings were rambling and often contradicted themselves. The word *gibberish*, which means "nonsense talk" is formed from his name.

A groundskeeper from the early twentieth century sprays arsenic acid onto a golf course. The arsenic was used to kill weeds and insects. Doing this would be illegal today because arsenic is so poisonous.

Pure arsenic

In 1250 Albertus Magnus (1193–1280), a German bishop, apparently produced pure arsenic. He seems to have done this by heating orpiment with soap, though the description of what he did is vague. Four hundred years later another German scientist, Johann Schröder (1600–1664), definitely obtained pure arsenic, by heating white arsenic (now known to be arsenic trioxide; As_2O_3) with charcoal. This is one of the main methods for purifying arsenic today.

Useful substance

As chemistry and industry progressed in the eighteenth and nineteenth centuries, many new uses were found for materials containing arsenic. It was used in purifying iron and in pigments for paints and fabric dyes. Arsenic's poisonous effects were known by this time, but no one knew just how dangerous the element was. For example, it was commonly used in face powders and creams. However, arsenic's poisonous properties were used to kill rats and mice in people's houses. It was sprayed on crops to kill insects and added to wood to prevent woodworm.

mercury. He also suggested that gold could be produced from other metals by eliminating the other "spirits," such as arsenic. Geber published this idea in around 800 C.E. It influenced alchemical thinking for several centuries.

Arsenic and crime

Napoleon Bonaparte was transported to the remote Atlantic island of St. Helena after being captured by the British in 1815. He died on the island six years later, perhaps as a result of arsenic poisoning.

Arsenic has been called "the king of poisons" because it has long been favored by murderers. It was used in ancient Rome where politicians often murdered each other. Much later, arsenic was called "inheritance powder," because giving it to a rich relative could bring you their wealth as an inheritance.

Possible murder

Some very famous people have been murdered with arsenic. One of them may have been the French emperor Napoleon Bonaparte (1769–1821). He died in exile on the island of St. Helena. Locks of his hair that have been preserved contain large amounts of arsenic. Some experts say he was poisoned, perhaps by agents of the French government. The new French leaders were afraid that Napoleon would one day return and take over France again.

Poisoners

There were many arsenic poisonings in the nineteenth century. Rat poison containing arsenic was easily available.

This bottle of arsenic acid was used as a poison. The poison killed pests, such as rats.

DISCOVERERS

The German chemist Robert Bunsen (1811–1899) is best known for inventing the small gas burner used in chemistry laboratories. Bunsen burners are used by chemists and high-school students even today. However, Bunsen also discovered an antidote to arsenic poisoning. An antidote is a medicine that stops a poison from working. Bunsen's antidote to arsenic poisoning was powdered iron oxide. This is still used to treat accidental arsenic poisoning.

Some murderers made poisons by boiling arsenic-coated flypaper in water. They then added this water to their victims' food or drink.

In 1871 the U.S. Navy's USS *Polaris* was anchored off Greenland, waiting for the spring thaw to melt the Arctic ice before it could continue its mission to the North Pole. One day, after drinking a mug of coffee with a strange taste, the ship's captain, Charles Hall, complained of pains and numbness. His symptoms got worse, and he was convinced he was being poisoned. He died after a few weeks. In 1968 his body was dug up and large amounts of arsenic were found.

In 1873 a British woman named Mary Cotton was hanged for murdering her stepson with arsenic. She also probably poisoned eight of her own children, six other stepchildren, three husbands, her mother, and a boyfriend in the same way.

How arsenic is produced

Arsenic compounds have been produced in many ways throughout history. Arsenic is rarely produced in a pure state. It is mainly extracted from its minerals by converting it into arsenic trioxide (As_2O_3), which is also called white arsenic.

Purifying arsenic

Arsenic atoms are relatively easy to remove from compounds. Heating most arsenic minerals, such as arsenopyrite or realgar, will cause the arsenic atoms to be released as a gas. This gas is sometimes collected and cooled down until it becomes solid arsenic. More often, the gas is reacted with oxygen to make white arsenic.

However, pure arsenic is a little harder to extract from white arsenic. The technique used is called smelting. The same method is used to purify many metals, such as iron. During arsenic smelting, white arsenic is heated with carbon. The carbon reacts with the oxygen in the white arsenic making carbon dioxide (CO_2) gas. Pure arsenic is left behind and collected.

Byproduct

A byproduct is something produced while a more important product is being made. Pure arsenic and arsenic oxide are rarely

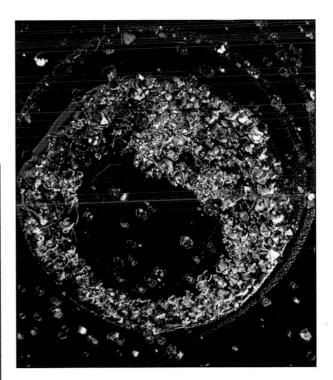

A view of pure arsenic crystals seen through a microscope. The colors are produced by light shining through the tiny and very thin crystals.

WHERE ARSENIC IS PRODUCED	
The amount of arsenic trioxide (As_2O_3) produced around of the world in 2003:	
China	17,637 tons (16,000 tonnes)
Chile	8,818 tons (8,000 tonnes)
Peru	3,307 tons (3,000 tonnes)
Mexico	2,205 tons (2,000 tonnes)
Kazakhstan	1,653 tons (1,500 tonnes
Russia	1,653 tons (1,500 tonnes)
Total:	38,680 tons (35,090 tonnes)

DID YOU KNOW?

POISONING THE PEARS

The Jibbinbar Mine in Queensland, Australia, was one of the few mines that was set up just to produce arsenic. The mine was opened in 1918 to make a powerful herbicide, or plant poison. The herbicide was used to kill prickly pears. This cactus had been introduced to Australia from South America in 1788, and it soon became a big problem. By 1918 it covered 50,000 square miles (130,000 km^2) of Queensland and was spreading over another 1,500 square miles (3,900 km^2) every year.

The mine made the herbicide by heating arsenopyrite, an ore made from arsenic, iron, and sulfur. The ore gave off arsenic gas and arsenic oxide dust. The dust was collected from the chimney and then sold to farmers. The mine closed in 1925 when less expensive herbicides were developed.

ATOMS AT WORK

When many arsenic minerals are heated, the arsenic atoms are released as a gas. For example, realgar molecules (arsenic sulfide; As_4S_4) are rings of four arsenic and four sulfur atoms. When it is heated the ring breaks up, and the atoms mix with the air.

Arsenic sulfide — Arsenic — Sulfur — Oxygen — Oxygen gas (O_2)

The arsenic and sulfur atoms react with the oxygen molecules in the air. The oxygen molecules first split into individual atoms.

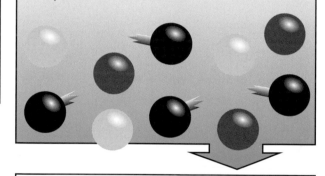

Arsenic forms arsenic trioxide (As_2O_3). When this cools down it forms white dust. The sulfur forms sulfur dioxide (SO_2), which is a strong-smelling gas.

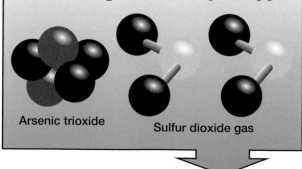

Arsenic trioxide   Sulfur dioxide gas

The reaction that takes place can be written like this:

$$As_4S_4 + 7O_2 \rightarrow 2As_2O_3 + 4SO_2$$

the main substances made at a chemical refinery. Instead they are byproducts made when metals such as gold, silver, copper, and lead are purified.

The way arsenic is separated from lead is typical of how it is made. The lead is melted in a furnace, and air is blasted through the liquid metal. Impurities, including arsenic, combine with oxygen in the air, and form a liquid called slag that floats on the lead. The slag is skimmed off. It contains arsenic oxides and other compounds. The arsenic is removed from the slag by smelting.

Chemistry of arsenic

Arsenic is useful because of the way it reacts with different elements and compounds. Arsenic reacts in these ways because of the structure of its atoms.

Thirty-three electrons circle the nucleus of the arsenic atom. Five of these electrons are located in the fourth and outermost shell. The five outer electrons determine how arsenic reacts. Arsenic atoms need three more electrons in their outer shell to become most stable. They react with other elements to take these electrons from atoms that want to lose electrons, such as metals. The arsenic atoms will also share the electrons they need with other atoms.

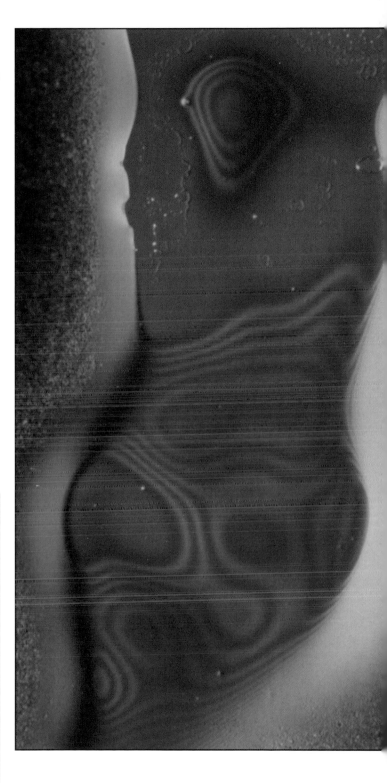

DID YOU KNOW?

SIMILAR SUBSTANCES

The element that is most similar to arsenic is phosphorus. Phosphorus has fifteen electrons, five of which are in its outer shell. Having the same number of outer electrons makes phosphorus and arsenic behave in similar ways. For example, both elements have more than one pure form. Arsenic exists in gray and yellow forms, while pure phosphorus is either red, white, or black. Both elements form ions with oxygen. These ions are called phosphates (PO_4^{3-}) and arsenates (AsO_4^{3-}) respectively. Phosphate ions are common in human bodies, but arsenate ions are poisonous to humans.

A close-up of realgar crystals as they melt. As the realgar melts, the arsenic atoms break away and are given off as pure arsenic gas.

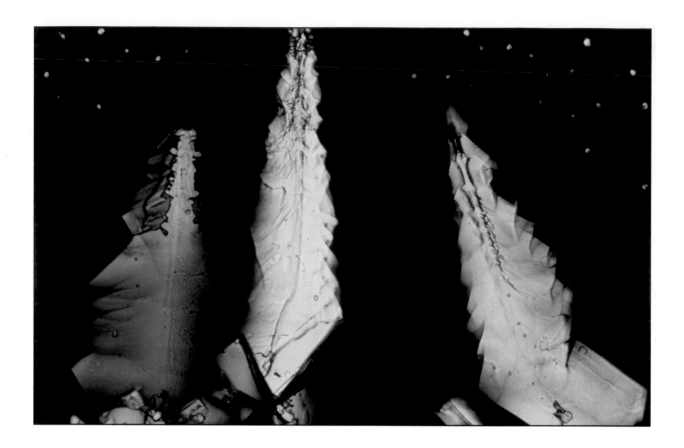

These arsenic sulfide crystals are viewed through a microscope. When heated, this compound reacts with oxygen in the air to make arsenic oxides.

Oxidation

Gray arsenic, the most common form of the element, is shiny like a metal. However, it tarnishes, which means that a thin surface layer forms on the solid arsenic after a few hours. This layer makes the surface dull. The dull coating is made of arsenic oxides, which form as the arsenic reacts with oxygen in the air.

This reaction speeds up if the arsenic is heated in air. The arsenic atoms combine with oxygen to form a mixture of two oxide compounds. One is arsenic trioxide (As_2O_3) or white arsenic. This compound is given that name because it forms as a cloud of white dust.

DID YOU KNOW?

SUBLIMATION

When solid arsenic is heated with no air present, it does not melt into a liquid, like ice melts into water. Instead, at 1135 °F (613 °C), arsenic sublimes, or turns directly from solid into gas. If arsenic is heated under very high pressure—twenty-eight times higher than the pressure of the atmosphere—it does melt. Under these conditions it turns into liquid at 1503 °F (817 °C).

The other substance formed when arsenic is heated in air is more complicated than white arsenic. It is called tetra-arsenic decaoxide. It consists of four atoms of arsenic combined with ten atoms of oxygen. The formula is As_4O_{10}.

Metal compounds

Arsenic combines with metals to form compounds called arsenides. An example is iron arsenide ($FeAs_2$). Arsenic is found combined with many different metals in rocks around the world. These compounds were made by chemical reactions that occurred millions of years ago, when the rocks formed deep inside the Earth.

ATOMS AT WORK

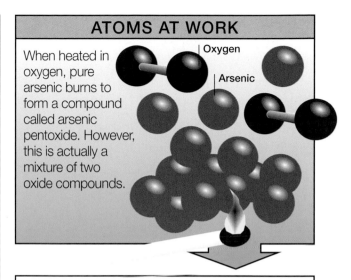

When heated in oxygen, pure arsenic burns to form a compound called arsenic pentoxide. However, this is actually a mixture of two oxide compounds.

Oxygen

Arsenic

The oxygen molecules break apart. The oxygen and arsenic atoms then combine. Some of the arsenic atoms form arsenic trioxide (As_2O_3), in which three oxygens combine with two arsenic atoms.

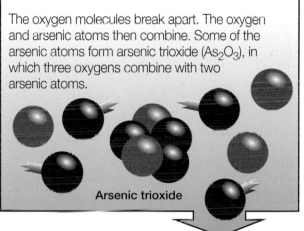

Arsenic trioxide

Other arsenic atoms form tetra-arsenic decaoxide (As_4O_{10}), in which ten oxygen atoms bond with four arsenic atoms. In mixtures of As_2O_3 and As_4O_{10} there are always five atoms of oxygen for every two of arsenic. Therefore the mixture is called arsenic pentoxide (As_2O_5).

Arsenic trioxide

Tetra-arsenic decaoxide

The reactions that take place can be written like this:
$$4As + 3O_2 \rightarrow 2As_2O_3$$
$$4As + 5O_2 \rightarrow As_4O_{10}$$

Modern uses of arsenic

By the beginning of the twentieth century, arsenic was being used in a variety of ways. Many of those uses have since been abandoned because scientists now know how poisonous arsenic compounds really are. For example, arsenic compounds were once commonly included in fireworks and distress flares. They helped to make loud bangs and clouds of smoke. Modern fireworks contain only tiny amounts of arsenic because too much might have bad effects on the environment or poison people watching the firework display.

Nevertheless the poisonous qualities of arsenic are still useful. Arsenic is used in pesticides (poisons used against damaging animals) and herbicides (poisons used against unwanted plants). There are strict rules to ensure that the people using these poisons and others in the area are not harmed.

Harmless amounts of arsenic are often added to glass to make it clear. Without arsenic in it the glass would have a pale yellow color.

Lead shot is packed into a shotgun cartridge. Arsenic is used to make the shot as spherical as possible. Round shot will fly in a straight line and it is easier to aim than uneven-shaped shot.

Purifying metals

Arsenic is used in producing certain metals. For example, platinum is a very tough and shiny metal that has a high melting point and does not rust. These properties make it very valuable but also make it difficult to separate from an ore. Platinum cannot be melted easily or reacted with other chemicals to separate it from the unwanted material in the ore. However, if arsenic is added, the platinum melts more easily and can be separated.

Industrial uses

Arsenic is also used in many processes where it is carefully contained so it does not harm the public. It is added to some metals, such as iron and copper, to make them harder. It is used in glass-making to remove unwanted colors from the glass. Just like centuries ago, arsenic is used in dyes to make bright, hard-wearing cloth.

Microchips

Some of the most modern high-tech industries use arsenic compounds. Microchips are made of materials called

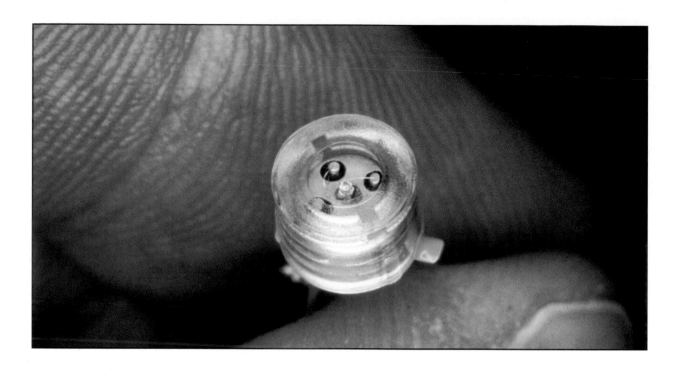

This diode contains the semiconductor gallium arsenide. The diode acts as a "valve" for electric current. It controls where the current flows through a circuit, so some components are on while others are off. This diode is actually very large for a modern semiconductor component. Diodes used in microchips are only visible using a microscope.

DID YOU KNOW?

SEMICONDUCTORS

A substance that allows an electric current to run through it is called a conductor. A substance that blocks electric currents is called an insulator. Semiconductors are substances that sometimes behave as good conductors and at other times they are good insulators. Whether they conduct or insulate depends on their temperature and the presence of tiny amounts of impurities. These impurities, which include arsenic, are called "doping agents." Some elements are semiconductors in their pure state, including silicon and germanium. Other semiconductors are compounds, such as gallium arsenide. In their pure form, neither arsenic or gallium are very good semiconductors.

Semiconductors are used to make electronic components that control devices such as computers. For examples, transistors are tiny switches that can alter the size of an electric current very quickly and precisely. Diodes are also made of semiconductors. They direct a current into certain parts of a circuit. The electronic components can be tiny. For example, there are many thousands of them on a single microchip.

semiconductors. These usually consist of elements such as silicon (Si) or germanium (Ge). Semiconductors are useful because they can be made to control electric currents in tiny and complex circuits. The circuits are cut into crystals of the semiconductor, but to work properly the semiconductors must be "doped," or have tiny quantities of other elements added. Arsenic is often used as the "doping agent." The arsenic is transferred into the semiconductor using jets of arsine (AsH_3) gas. This consists of arsenic and hydrogen and is extremely dangerous because it is not only poisonous but also explodes easily.

Lasers

Another very useful semiconductor is gallium arsenide (GaAs). This is used to make very fast-acting electronic circuits. Gallium arsenide microchips are several times faster than silicon chips. Gallium arsenide can also be used to convert electricity directly into light. For example, it is used in the screens of small handheld electronic devices, such as cell phones and portable media players.

Gallium arsenide is used to make tiny lasers that convert electric signals into pulses of light. These are used to send information along optical fibers, such as those inside communication cables. The same type of laser is used to read laser discs, such as DVDs (Digital Versatile Disc).

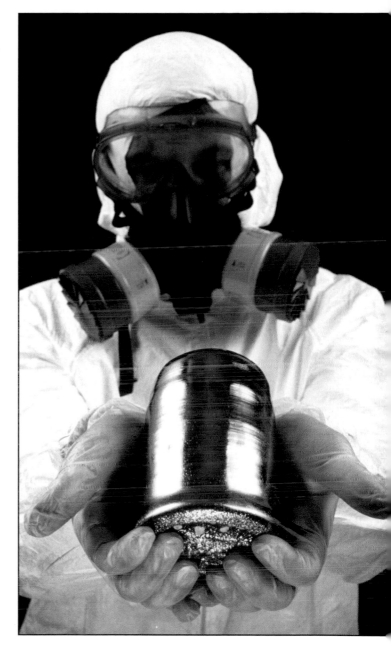

A technician holds a piece of the semiconductor gallium arsenide. This is a compound of arsenic and the metal gallium. The technician is wearing a mask because gallium arsenide is poisonous. However, the mask, gloves, and bodysuit are also used to help keep the compound very clean because any dirt will stop it from working as a semiconductor.

Arsenic and health

It is strange to think that a deadly substance such as arsenic was used to help people recover from diseases. However, an arsenic-containing medicine called Fowler's Solution was invented in 1780 and was used until the 1960s. The people who took it claimed to feel better, and it was also thought to have good effects on skin diseases. However, it

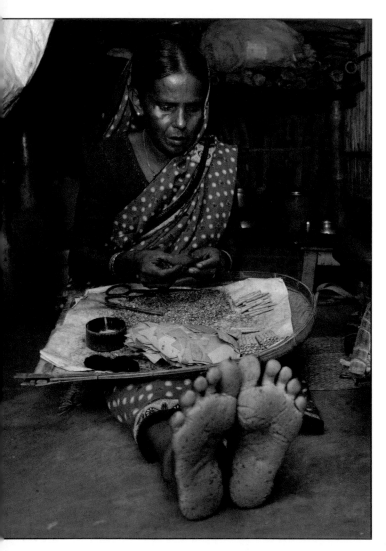

probably also had a damaging effect on the body. This and other risky potions invented in the nineteenth century were eventually replaced by modern medicines, such as antibiotics, which fight bacteria and other infectious organisms.

However, one arsenic-containing medicine called Salvarsan certainly did a lot of good. It was invented by the German bacteriologist Paul Ehrlich (1854–1915). Ehrlich decided to find out whether arsenic could be used against the tiny organisms that cause the deadly disease syphilis. He added arsenic to many different molecules and tried to produce a substance that would attack the disease

A woman poisoned by drinking water contaminated with arsenic in India in 2004. The arsenic has produced sores on her feet.

and not the patient. He was successful in 1909. He called this new drug "Salvarsan." Salvarsan was also effective against other diseases, including African sleeping sickness. The drug was the first compound to be designed to work as a medicine. Today all medicines are developed in a similar way to target a particular disease. By the 1940s, however, Salvarsan was being replaced by the antibiotic penicillin, which worked more quickly.

This kit for administering Salvarsan was used in the early twentieth century.

Today arsenic is again being used in medicine. In 2003 the U.S. Food and Drug Administration allowed arsenic trioxide to be tested as a possible treatment for leukemia—a cancer that affects the blood.

Environmental hazard

In the past, metal refineries spread huge clouds of arsenic-containing smoke and dust over the surrounding countryside. Although the emissions of arsenic have now been reduced, some soil will be contaminated for many years to come.

Emergency workers in China pour lime (calcium hydroxide) into a river to remove arsenic compounds. The arsenic entered the river in 2002 when half a ton of it was spilled from a truck.

One example is in King County, Washington. Local residents there are advised on how to test their soil to find out how much arsenic it contains. This ensures that they can avoid being contaminated.

At Yellowknife, in Canada's Northwest Territories, the arsenic-containing dust from a gold smelter was collected in the smokestack to prevent it from polluting the environment. Now there are a quarter of a million tons of the dust stored underground. The material must either be sealed up forever or brought to the surface so the arsenic can be extracted and sold to pay for part of the cost of making the site safe.

Timber for building was often treated with arsenic to protect it from termites and other pests. This wood becomes especially dangerous when it is burned. Many people do not realize that the ash and smoke is poisonous. There have been cases of people falling ill after burning arsenic-treated wood in their houses.

Deadly wells

The greatest environmental threat involving arsenic has been caused by people who were actually trying to save the lives of the poor in southern Asia. Many people in this region do not have clean, running water. At the end of the twentieth century charities dug many deep wells in India and Bangladesh to provide water for as many people as possible. The wells were very deep and tapped water that was free of harmful microorganisms that often cause illnesses.

However, lots of people did get sick. The well water contained small but dangerous amounts of arsenic from the rocks deep underground. The effects on their health are only showing up now in people who have been drinking the water for years. Unfortunately, 100 million people have been exposed to the contaminated water, and it is likely that many of them will die before clean water can be provided.

DID YOU KNOW?

THE ICEMAN

Oetzi the Iceman, whose body was found in the Italian Alps in 1991, lived more than 5,000 years ago. He had high levels of arsenic inside his hair. But he froze to death and did not die from poisoning, so it is likely that he was a coppersmith. The arsenic got into his body as he made pure copper from ores also containing arsenic minerals.

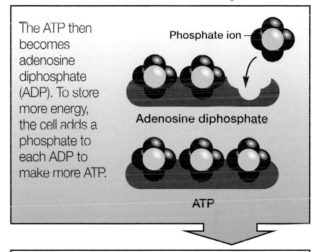

ATOMS AT WORK

One of the ways arsenic poisons people is by blocking the way the cells in the body store energy. When the cell needs energy, a molecule of adenosine triphosphate (ATP) releases one phosphate ion (PO_4^{3-}). This also releases energy.

Phosphate ion

Adenosine triphosphate

Oxygen

Phosphorus

The ATP then becomes adenosine diphosphate (ADP). To store more energy, the cell adds a phosphate to each ADP to make more ATP.

Phosphate ion

Adenosine diphosphate

ATP

If there is an arsenic atom in the cell, it blocks the phosphate by joining to the ADP in its place as an arsenate ion (AsO_4^{3-}). This stops the cell from being able to store the energy it needs to stay alive, and eventually the cell dies. If there is a lot of arsenic in the body, so many cells die that the whole body cannot survive.

Arsenate ion

Release of energy is now blocked.

ADP

Periodic table

Everything in the universe is made from combinations of substances called elements. Elements are made of tiny atoms, which are too small to see. Atoms are the building blocks of matter.

The character of an atom depends on how many even tinier particles called protons there are in its center, or nucleus. An element's atomic number is the same as the number of its protons.

Scientists have found around 116 different elements. About 90 elements occur naturally on Earth. The rest have been made in experiments.

All these elements are set out on a chart called the periodic table. This lists all the elements in order according to their atomic number.

The elements at the left of the table are metals. Those at the right are nonmetals. Between the metals and the nonmetals are the metalloids, which sometimes act like metals and sometimes like nonmetals.

● On the left of the table are the alkali metals. These have just one outer electron.

● Metals get more reactive as you go down a group. The most reactive nonmetals are at the top of the table.

● On the right of the periodic table are the noble gases. These elements have full outer shells.

● The number of electrons orbiting the nucleus increases down each group.

● Elements in the same group have the same number of electrons in their outer shells.

● The transition metals are in the middle of the table, between Groups II and III.

Group I

| 1 H Hydrogen 1 |

Group II

| 3 Li Lithium 7 | 4 Be Beryllium 9 |
| 11 Na Sodium 23 | 12 Mg Magnesium 24 |

Transition metals

19 K Potassium 39	20 Ca Calcium 40	21 Sc Scandium 45	22 Ti Titanium 48	23 V Vanadium 51	24 Cr Chromium 52	25 Mn Manganese 55	26 Fe Iron 56	27 Co Cobalt 59
37 Rb Rubidium 85	38 Sr Strontium 88	39 Y Yttrium 89	40 Zr Zirconium 91	41 Nb Niobium 93	42 Mo Molybdenum 96	43 Tc Technetium (98)	44 Ru Ruthenium 101	45 Rh Rhodium 103
55 Cs Cesium 133	56 Ba Barium 137	71 Lu Lutetium 175	72 Hf Hafnium 179	73 Ta Tantalum 181	74 W Tungsten 184	75 Re Rhenium 186	76 Os Osmium 190	77 Ir Iridium 192
87 Fr Francium 223	88 Ra Radium 226	103 Lr Lawrencium (260)	104 Rf Rutherfordium (263)	105 Db Dubnium (265)	106 Sg Seaborgium (266)	107 Bh Bohrium (272)	108 Hs Hassium (277)	109 Mt Meitnerium (276)

Lanthanide elements

| 57 La Lanthanum 39 | 58 Ce Cerium 140 | 59 Pr Praseodymium 141 | 60 Nd Neodymium 144 | 61 Pm Promethium (145) |

Actinide elements

| 89 Ac Actinium 227 | 90 Th Thorium 232 | 91 Pa Protactinium 231 | 92 U Uranium 238 | 93 Np Neptunium (237) |

The horizontal rows are called periods. As you go across a period, the atomic number increases by one from each element to the next. The vertical columns are called groups. Elements get heavier as you go down a group. All the elements in a group have the same number of electrons in their outer shells. This means they react in similar ways.

The transition metals fall between Groups II and III. Their electron shells fill up in an unusual way. The lanthanide elements and the actinide elements are set apart from the main table to make it easier to read. All the lanthanide elements and the actinide elements are quite rare.

Arsenic in the table

Arsenic is in group five (V) of the table. This is an unusual group because it contains nonmetals, metals, and metalloids. As a metalloid, arsenic has both the physical and chemical properties of metals and nonmetals. Since it is near the middle of the table, arsenic reacts with both metals and nonmetals.

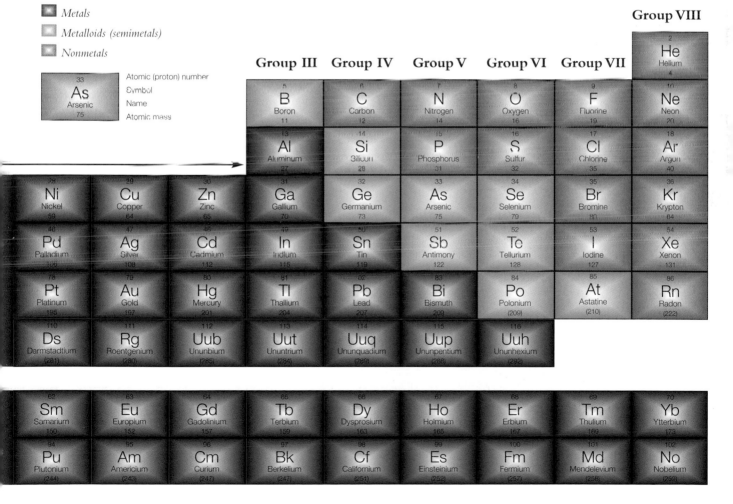

Chemical reactions

Chemical reactions are going on around us all the time. Some reactions involve just two substances, while others involve many more. But whenever a reaction takes place, at least one substance is changed. In a chemical reaction, the number and type of atoms stay the same. But they join up in different combinations to form new molecules.

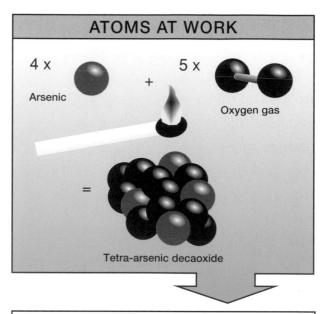

ATOMS AT WORK

4 x
Arsenic
+
5 x
Oxygen gas

=

Tetra-arsenic decaoxide

The reactions that take place can be written like this:

$$4As + 5O_2 \rightarrow As_4O_{10}$$

Tiny amounts of arsenic compounds are sometimes added to fireworks. When the fireworks explode, the arsenic reacts with oxygen to make a bright flash.

Writing an equation

Chemical reactions can be described by writing down the atoms and molecules before and after the reaction. Since the atoms stay the same, the number of atoms before will be the same as the number of atoms after. Chemists write the reaction as an equation. This shows what happens in the chemical reaction.

Making it balance

When the numbers of each atom on both sides of the equation are equal, the equation is balanced. If the numbers are not equal, something is wrong. So the chemist adjusts the number of atoms involved until the equation is balanced.

Glossary

atom: The smallest part of an element having all the properties of that element.

atomic mass number: The number of protons and neutrons in an atom.

atomic number: The number of protons in an atom.

bond: The attraction between two atoms, or ions, that holds them together.

compound: A substance made of atoms of two or more elements. The atoms are held together by chemical bonds.

crystal: A solid consisting of a repeating pattern of atoms, ions, or molecules.

doping agent: A substance that is added in tiny amounts to semiconductors to improve the way they work. Arsenic is a common doping agent.

electron: A tiny particle with a negative charge. Electrons are found inside atoms, where they move around the nucleus in layers called electron shells.

element: A substance that is made from only one type of atom.

ion: An atom or a group of atoms that has lost or gained electrons to become electrically charged.

isotopes: Atoms of an element with the same number of protons and electrons but different numbers of neutrons.

mineral: A compound or element as it is found in its natural form in Earth.

metal: An element on the left-hand side of the periodic table.

metalloid: An element located in the middle of the periodic table that has properties of both metals and nonmetals. Arsenic is a metalloid.

nonmetal: An element on the left-hand side of the periodic table.

nucleus: The dense structure at the center of an atom. Protons and neutrons are found inside the nucleus of an atom.

neutron: A tiny particle with no electrical charge. Neutrons are found in the nucleus of almost every atom.

ore: A mineral or rock that contains enough of a particular substance to make it useful for mining.

periodic table: A chart of all the chemical elements laid out in order of their atomic number.

proton: A tiny particle with a positive charge. Protons are found in the nucleus.

radioactivity: A property of certain unstable atoms that causes them to release radiation.

reaction: A process in which two or more elements or compounds combine to produce new substances.

semiconductor: A substance that is sometimes a good conductor of electricity and sometimes a poor conductor of electricity.

solution: A liquid that has another substance dissolved in it.

Index